House of Screams!

"Prove that you're not scared," Joe dared his older brother. "Go up and ring the bell."

For a second Frank stood, not sure. But he wasn't going to let Joe think he was afraid.

"Out of my way," Frank said. He marched right up to the door. Then he pressed his finger against the bell, hard.

The bell sounded like an organ in an old monster movie.

Frank and Joe held their breath.

Then came the sound—a horrible bloodcurdling scream!

Frank and Joe Hardy: The Clues Brothers

Available from MINSTREL BOOKS

FRANK AND JOE HARDY: THE CLUES BROTHERS™

The GROSS GHOST MYSTERY

Franklin W. Dixon

Illustrated by
Frank Bolle

A MINSTREL® BOOK

Published by POCKET BOOKS
New York   London   Toronto   Sydney   Tokyo   Singapore

This book is a work of fiction. Names, characters, places and incidents are products of the author's imagination or are used fictitiously. Any resemblance to actual events or locales or persons, living or dead, is entirely coincidental.

A MINSTREL PAPERBACK *Original*

 A Minstrel Book published by
POCKET BOOKS, a division of Simon & Schuster Inc.
1230 Avenue of the Americas, New York, NY 10020

Copyright © 1997 by Simon & Schuster Inc.

Produced by Mega-Books, Inc.

Front cover illustration by Thompson Studio

ISBN: 0-671-00402-6

First Minstrel Books printing September 1997

10 9 8 7 6 5 4 3 2 1

FRANK AND JOE HARDY: THE CLUES BROTHERS is a trademark of Simon & Schuster Inc.

THE HARDY BOYS, A MINSTREL BOOK and colophon are registered trademarks of Simon & Schuster Inc.

Printed in the U.S.A.

1

Ghosts, Ghouls, and Eyeballs

Finished!" Joe Hardy yelled, charging out of his new room. "I unpacked everything, Frank. It was easy!"

Joe almost crashed into his brother, Frank, who came puffing up the stairs. He gave Joe a dirty look over the big box in his arms. "Sure it was. You only unpacked one box."

Joe shrugged. "Big deal. I got out all the good stuff. Check it out."

The best thing about their new house was that each brother had his own room.

They wouldn't have to draw chalk lines down the middle of the floor anymore.

When Frank looked into Joe's room, he nearly dropped the box. "Mom is going to kill you," he said. "This place is crawling with your dumb monster toys!"

"They're not toys," Joe said. "It's my collection of the grossest stuff on earth."

Joe's slimy worms, jellied eyeballs, and slippery slugs were strewn all over his room.

His favorite figure sat on the night table beside his bed. It was a wiggly ghost made of milky white plastic, and it had fangs, claws, and two extra arms that looked like snakes. Joe picked it up and stuck it in Frank's face.

"Mwah-ha, ha." Joe gave an evil laugh.

Frank pretended to shiver. "Ooooh— I'm soooo scared!" he said.

Joe frowned. Frank was always making fun of his stuff.

Frank dumped the box he was carrying on Joe's bed. "Hurry up and finish so we can go out and explore."

"Hey, watch it! You almost stepped on my Super Slimer." Joe carefully picked up the figure that Frank had knocked over. "I was just about to put it up there."

Joe pointed to the top shelf of his book-case. He jumped up on the bed. Even when he stood on tiptoe, the shelf was too high for him to reach. The slimer slipped out of his hands, and Frank caught it in midair.

"Move over, shrimp," Frank said. He climbed up, stretched, and put the figure in place.

Frank was nine, only a year older than Joe. And only a little taller.

"Show-off!"

"Race you down the stairs," Frank yelled. He jumped off the bed and ran. Joe followed him.

"Rotten egg," Frank said when he reached the bottom first.

Mrs. Hardy was hanging a shade on one of the kitchen windows.

"Mom, can we go outside?" Frank asked.

"That depends," Mrs. Hardy said. "Did you finish unpacking your boxes?"

"Just about," Joe said quickly.

Frank rolled his eyes.

"Okay, have fun," Mrs. Hardy said. "But be home in an hour for dinner."

Outside, Joe peered up and down the street. "So where are the stores?"

When they lived in New York City, they never had to walk more than a block to find a store. There were all sorts of shops—delis, dry cleaners, fruit stands. Here in Bayport, there was nothing but houses and trees.

"Let's try this way," Frank said, pointing to the right.

They walked for a while but saw only houses and lawns and cars parked in driveways. It was the end of the summer, two weeks before school started. The whole neighborhood was quiet.

"I just had a scary thought, Frank," Joe said. "What if we're the only kids in this whole town?"

Frank thought for a moment. "If we *are* the only kids, think of all the candy we'll get on Halloween."

Then Frank heard laughter from down the street. Several boys had turned a corner and were running ahead of them.

"Look, there are some kids! I guess we'll have to share the candy after all," Frank said.

But Joe wasn't listening. He was busy staring at a huge mansion across the street.

"Hey, Frank," Joe said, nudging his brother with his elbow. "Speaking of Halloween, look at that house!"

The old house must have been two times the size of the Hardys' house. It was brownish gray, and its paint was peeling.

It had lots of windows, but most of them were broken or boarded up. The run-down mansion was surrounded by a black iron fence with spikes on top.

Frank whistled. "Wow."

"I bet it's haunted," Joe whispered.

"No way," Frank said.

"Yes way!" Joe insisted. "And it's probably filled with ghosts!"

Frank shook his head. "Look at this place, Joe. No one has lived here for years."

"Who said anything about *living?* Ghosts are supposed to be *dead*, Frank, remember?" Joe said.

"Give me a break!" Frank said.

Joe crossed the street and walked over to the gate. When he pushed, the gate opened with a creak. Then it fell off.

Joe glanced at his brother. "You coming?"

Frank looked unhappily at the house. I don't know—"

"You're scared," Joe said. He walked through the gate. "I may be younger than you, but I'm braver."

"Who said I was scared?" Frank demanded. He followed Joe.

"Prove that you're not," Joe dared his older brother. "Go up and ring the bell."

For a second Frank stood, not sure. But he wasn't going to let Joe think he was afraid.

"Out of my way," Frank said. He marched right up to the door. Then he pressed his finger against the bell, hard.

The bell sounded like an organ in an old monster movie.

Frank and Joe held their breath.

Then came the sound—a horrible bloodcurdling scream!

2

No Such Thing

Frank gulped. He took his finger off the bell. But the screaming got louder!

He glanced back at Joe, who looked ready to run. Frank knew how he felt. He was ready to run, too.

Suddenly the front door flew open. A chubby blond kid about their age came barreling out, screaming at the top of his lungs. He knocked Frank down and rammed into Joe.

"What's the big idea?" Frank shouted, getting to his feet.

"You could have flattened me, too," Joe added.

The boy apologized. "S-sorry about that. It's just that I was in a hurry."

The boy's face was completely white, except for his freckles.

"Wow! You look like you've seen a ghost," Joe said. He grabbed the boy by the arm. "Did you?"

"Not exactly. But this house *is* haunted. Everybody in Bayport knows that."

Joe glanced at Frank. "See? I told you."

Frank turned to the boy.

"We just moved here," Frank explained. "I'm Frank Hardy. This is my brother, Joe."

"I'm Chet—Chet Morton," the boy said, introducing himself.

"If that house is haunted, what were you doing in there?" Joe wanted to know.

"Well, it's kind of a long story," Chet said. "I was having a snack at the playground—a tuna fish sandwich. Some guys grabbed my baseball glove and started throwing it back and forth. Then they ran off with it."

"Did you go after them?" Frank asked.

"I started to," Chet continued. "But then I dropped my potato chips. When I bent down to pick them up, my candy bar fell out of my jacket pocket."

"Wow, all that for a snack?" Joe asked.

"Yeah, you must love to eat," Frank said.

Chet shrugged. "It's not that much."

"What happened to the guys who took your glove?" Frank wanted to know.

"After I picked up the candy bar, I couldn't see where they went."

"That still doesn't tell us why you were in the house," Frank said.

"After a while they came back to the playground. They told me they threw my glove into this haunted house." Chet jammed his hands into his pockets.

"Bummer," Joe said.

"They said I was too chicken to go inside. But I wasn't scared. So I came over here and I went in."

"Then what happened?" Frank asked.

Joe's eyes opened wide. "Yeah. Then what happened?"

"It was really dark in there. I tripped and hit my head on the wall. Then I heard something."

"What?" Joe asked.

"A sort of scraping noise. When I turned toward the sound, I saw—"

"A slimy-looking guy with fangs and claws? And arms that look like snakes?" Joe said.

Frank jabbed Joe with his elbow. Did Joe really expect to find ghosts in there?

"I didn't see anything—except a pair of eyes," Chet said. "Glowing red eyes. They were staring at me."

Joe's mouth fell open. "What did you do?"

"I screamed," Chet said. "Then I ran. Then I bumped into you guys."

"But you told us you weren't scared," Joe said.

"I wasn't," Chet insisted. "Well, not totally."

Chet sat down on the doorstep. He

rested his chin in his hands. "But my glove is still in there, and it's brand-new. I just got it for my birthday."

Frank looked at Joe. Joe looked at Frank. "Maybe we should go in and check it out," Frank offered.

"W-we?" Chet asked with a gulp.

"Joe and I will go in," Frank explained. "You stay outside and keep watch."

Chet nodded gratefully. "Good idea." He pulled a candy bar from his pocket, ripped off the paper, and took a bite.

Frank stepped up to the open door. Joe was right behind him.

"Cool!" Joe said. "We're going to see a ghost."

"Shhh," Frank said. "If there *are* ghosts in there, your voice will scare them away. Anyway, we're not going to see any ghosts because there's no such thing."

"What about the glowing red eyes that Chet saw?" Joe asked. "Sounds pretty creepy to me."

"Joe, remember when you were a little

kid?" Frank said. "You thought you saw a big snake with glowing red eyes in the living room. But it was just the VCR."

Joe could feel his face turn bright red. "That never happened!"

"Did, too!"

"Did not!"

As the boys moved away from the door, the hallway got darker and darker. Frank wished he had a flashlight. He squinted into the darkness. There had to be a door-way to another room somewhere.

"Stay in front of me, Joe. That way we won't get lost."

The boys inched their way down the dark hallway.

"Frank! Frank! Something is breathing down my neck!" Joe cried.

"It's me, dweeb. Keep walking."

The boys stepped carefully, slowly. "It looks like there's a doorway over here," Frank said.

There was. They stepped into what seemed like a big room. Dim light came from a broken, partly boarded-up window.

Crunch!

Joe jumped. "Frank, I think I stepped on a pile of bones!"

"It's probably glass from the broken window. Be careful," Frank said.

Frank wrinkled his nose as he headed for the window. "Gross!" he said. "This place smells worse than your feet."

Thick, heavy curtains covered most of the window. Frank pulled them aside to let in more light.

Joe blinked. When he could see, he pointed to a clean spot on the dusty floor. "Something was here," he said.

Frank looked at the spot. Then he looked around the large room. It was full of furniture covered with dusty white sheets.

Joe whistled. "Let's check for ghosts."

Frank peeked under some of the sheets. "No ghosts here. Just an old chair, a lumpy sofa. And a—a—a—"

"Frank, what is it?" Joe asked.

"A *skeleton!*" Frank shouted.

3

No Bones About It

Joe yanked at the sheet. It fluttered to the floor. Swinging on an iron stand was a gleaming white skeleton with a toothy grin. Its bony arms flapped as it swayed back and forth.

Joe turned to run. "I'm out of here!" he shouted.

"Wait for me!" Frank yelled.

This time Frank and Joe almost knocked Chet down as they ran from the house.

"What did you find?" Chet asked.

"Oh, not much," Frank said, gasping

for air. "Just some broken glass, a lot of dust—and a skeleton."

"A skeleton?" Chet's eyes opened wide. "Was it wearing my baseball glove?"

Frank shook his head quickly.

"I knew this place was haunted," Joe said. "Why else would a skeleton be hanging around in there?"

"Chill out," Frank said. "Just because there's a skeleton in the house doesn't mean it's haunted."

"How do you know?" Chet asked.

"My teacher in New York kept a skeleton in our classroom," Frank explained.

"So what?" Joe said.

"All I'm saying is that there might be a reason for the skeleton to be in there."

Chet frowned. "Yeah. Like maybe Zack planted him there."

"Who's Zack?" Frank asked.

"The leader of the guys who ran off with my glove," Chet explained. "Zack Jackson is a big-time bully. He always gets other kids to do his dirty work, just like he did this time."

"Don't worry," Frank spoke up. "We'll help you find your glove."

"Yeah," Joe said.

"How?" Chet asked.

"Well, our dad is a detective. He used to work for the New York City Police Department."

"Cool. Your dad's a cop? Can he help, too?" Chet asked.

"Well, he's not a cop anymore, but we can ask him for advice," Frank said.

"But we don't really need his help," Joe bragged. "Frank and I are pretty good detectives ourselves."

"We are?" Frank said.

"Yeah, we work as a team."

"We do?" Frank said.

"Sure," Joe answered. "This'll be our first real case, though. Come on, Frank, we can solve it."

Frank nodded. "Of course we can."

Chet was quiet for a moment. Then he shrugged. "Why not?"

"We can ask Dad for some ideas when

we get home," Frank said. He looked at his watch. "We'd better get going."

Chet told the Hardys how to get to the playground, and they agreed to meet him there the next morning. Then the brothers headed home.

The boys were just starting to set the table for dinner when their father came in carrying a big bag. "See what a great detective I am?" He laughed. "I found a Chinese restaurant two blocks from my new office."

"Way to go, Dad!" Joe said. He loved Chinese food as much as his father did.

"Did you boys meet any kids in the neighborhood?" Mrs. Hardy asked once they had all helped themselves.

"Just one," Joe announced. He speared a piece of broccoli with a chopstick. "But something even better happened. We went into a haunted house and saw a skeleton!"

"A skeleton?" Mrs. Hardy repeated.

"Are you sure?" Mr. Hardy asked.

Frank kicked Joe lightly under the table. He didn't want their mom and dad to keep them from solving the case.

"That house was really dark," Frank said. "The skeleton could have been a hat rack."

"Made out of bones," Joe added quietly.

Fenton Hardy listened as Frank told the story of Chet's baseball mitt. Joe added some details.

"So you boys think someone took the glove out of the house?" Mr. Hardy said.

"Stole it, you mean," Joe said.

"What would you do, Dad?" Frank asked.

"I'd start with basic detective work," Mr. Hardy said. "That means checking the scene for clues. I'd also make a list of suspects—people who might have wanted the glove."

Joe nodded. He grabbed a fortune cookie and cracked it open.

"What does it say?" Frank asked.

Joe read his fortune. He looked up and stared at Frank. "It says, 'Where there is curiosity, there is danger.' "

"Uh-oh," Frank said.

Later that evening Frank turned on the family computer. He typed the word "Clues" on the empty screen.

"We don't have any clues," Joe said.

Frank ignored him. He was busy labeling another screen "Suspects."

"How can we have suspects when we don't know anybody here?" Joe asked, standing at Frank's elbow.

"We have one suspect," Frank said, carefully typing in the name *Zack*. He frowned. "A good mystery story usually has three suspects."

"But this isn't a story—it's real life," Joe said. "What if whoever stole the glove isn't even alive? What if it's a ghost?"

"Will you quit it already?" Frank wailed. "We're going to limit this list to real-live people, okay? And tomorrow we might find more suspects at the playground."

But Joe leaned over the keyboard and typed "The ghost."

"Now we have two suspects," he said.

Frank sighed, then saved the file and turned off the power. "Till tomorrow," he said.

The next morning Mrs. Hardy dropped the boys off at the playground. Chet stood waiting for them at the gate.

"Wow!" Joe said after waving goodbye to his mother. "This is great!"

The playground was part of a park that took up several blocks. From the car Frank and Joe had seen a baseball field, basketball courts, even a path for skating.

"This place *is* excellent," Chet agreed. "But look who's coming—Zack and his pals Mark and Brett. I don't know who the other guy is."

Four boys walked toward them. The leader was shorter than Joe, but he looked mean. As he came closer, Joe saw that he had wild black hair and a skinny, pointy face. The other guys were bigger.

"Hi, Zack," Chet muttered to the small kid.

Zack Jackson had a big voice and a loud laugh. "Hey, is that Chet Morton, or did the elephant escape from the zoo? Ha-ha-ha!"

Frank realized he had heard that laughter before. It had come from one of the boys running past the haunted house.

"So, Chunky." Zack punched Chet on the shoulder. "Did you find your stupid glove?"

"The way we heard it, you stole the glove," Joe said.

Zack frowned at Chet. Then he gave the Hardys a wide, phony grin. "Is that what Chet told you?"

Chet folded his arms across his chest. "Maybe I did."

"Well, you're wrong," Zack sneered. "You lost the glove. After all, you *are* a natural-born loser! Ha-ha-ha!"

"Very funny," Chet mumbled.

"We *found* the glove," Zack insisted. "Then we left it where it would be safe— guarded by ghouls. Right, Biff?"

A huge blond kid standing behind Zack nodded. "Right, Zack."

"Biff?" Joe laughed. "What kind of a dopey name is that?"

Biff's face turned red. He stepped forward to loom over Joe.

"Everybody calls me Biff. Know why?" He made a fist and punched his palm. "That's the sound of what happens to kids I don't like. *Biff! Biff!*" He shoved Joe really hard.

But Joe knew how to handle bullies. Even though he had to reach up to do it, he swung his fist.

"Pleased to meet you . . . Biff!"
Smack!

With one punch, Joe slugged Biff right in the nose!

4

The Zack Pack

Owwww!" Biff yelled. He reeled back. Then he fell right on his butt.

"My nose!" He clamped both hands across his face and stared up at Joe.

"Come on, Biff," Frank said. "He didn't hit you that hard."

But Mark and Brett, the other kids with Zack, stared, too.

"Everybody saw that!" Zack shouted.

"What did you do that for?" Mark asked.

"Yeah, you socked Biff for no reason!" Brett added.

Biff scrambled to his feet. His nose did look big and red.

"You'll be sorry!" Zack threatened. He walked away. The rest of his gang followed him.

Sure, Frank thought. Now he's far enough away to feel safe. He watched Zack and his friends quickly disappear into the park.

Joe stared down at his fist.

"That was awesome!" Chet cried.

A boy who had been playing nearby walked over. He was about the Hardys' age with black hair and dark skin. His eyes sparkled as he gave Joe a high five.

"Way to go!" he said. "I'm Mike Mendez."

"Hi, Mike," Frank said. "I'm Frank Hardy, and the guy with magic fists is my younger brother, Joe."

"This park used to be great," Mike said. "Until it was invaded by the Zack Pack."

Chet laughed. "The Zack Pack. That's good!"

"Well, the Zack Pack threw Chet's new mitt into the big haunted house on Oak Street," Joe said. "Now it's missing."

"I don't know if the house is haunted," Mike said. "But it *is* weird. My grandpa used to work there."

Frank turned to Mike. "Maybe your grandfather could tell us what he knows about the house."

"Sure, let's go ask him," Mike said. "He lives on Oak Street, on the same block as the old house."

Mike led the way. Soon they reached the haunted house. Mike passed it and walked on to the corner. The other boys followed.

A little house stood behind a thick green hedge. A thin man with leathery skin and white hair was gardening in the front yard.

"Grandpa!" Mike called.

The man turned and smiled. *"Hola!"* he said.

"Grandpa, meet Frank and Joe Hardy. They just moved to Bayport," Mike said.

"Hello, boys. I'm José Mendez," Mike's grandfather said. He glanced at Chet.

"And this is Chet Morton, from my school."

"Some kids took my new baseball glove," Chet said. "Then they threw it into the haunted house."

"You mean the Morrow mansion?" Mr. Mendez shook his head. "It was a beautiful place once. The Morrow family built that house more than a hundred years ago. I worked there for a long time."

"What happened to it?" Frank asked.

"After old Dr. Morrow's son, Robert, died, no one wanted to live there. Robert was a doctor, too, a brain surgeon."

"See, Joe?" Frank said. "I knew there was a reason that skeleton was there."

"Did you ever see any ghosts when you worked there?" Joe asked, ignoring his brother.

Mr. Mendez chuckled. "There was always talk about the house being haunted. But I never believed it."

"Neither do I," Frank insisted.

"You can read all about the Morrow mansion," Mr. Mendez said. "When the house turned a hundred years old, the newspaper carried a long article about it."

"That's a good idea," Frank said. "But first we want to go back to the house and check it out."

Joe and Chet stared at Frank.

"We do?" they asked together.

Mr. Mendez put down his hedge clipper and began walking to a small shed. "It must be pretty dark in there. You'd better borrow my flashlight. And be careful!"

Minutes later the four boys were walking up the overgrown path to the Morrow mansion.

"Do we really want to go inside again?" Chet asked.

"Do you want your glove back or not?" Frank said.

"Of course I want it. My mom will kill me if she finds out I lost it already."

"Then come on."

Mike held his grandfather's flashlight out in front of him.

"What we need is a ghost-tracking device," he said as Frank opened the door.

"A what?" Joe asked.

"You know, something to spot and trap ghosts. I could build one," Mike explained.

"Mike's great at building machines and rigging stuff," Chet explained. "You should have seen the cool robot he made for our science fair."

The boys walked through the doorway and into the house.

"What's that smell?" Chet asked.

"Maybe it's a dead body," Joe said.

"Maybe it's your feet," Frank said. He led the way to the big room he and Joe had been in before. "Mike, shine the flashlight against that wall."

Mike aimed the beam at the wall. The

boys could see a gigantic fireplace covered with cobwebs. Above it hung a huge portrait of a man. The man had thick white hair and wore a long black cape.

"That must be Dr. Morrow!" Joe cried. "Look, he's got a brain in his hand!"

Frank moved closer to the portrait. "That's not a brain—it's a kitten!"

Mike shone the light on the cat. It was curled up in the doctor's hand. "Aw! It's cute!"

Chet took the flashlight from Mike. "Forget the cat, you guys. Let's look for my glove."

The boys moved on. Joe was sure the eyes in the portrait were following him.

The boys spread out as Chet aimed the flashlight across the dusty floor.

"Footprints!" Chet exclaimed.

The circle of light rested on several blurred scratches.

"They're small," Joe said. "Maybe a little kid made them."

"Or a skeleton," Frank said.

"These scratches must have been made by the skeleton you saw!" Chet exclaimed. "If *he* stole the glove, maybe we should let him keep it."

"Where do the footprints go?" Joe asked. "Shine the light down there." He grabbed Chet's arm, trying to aim the light along the floor.

The boys bumped into Mike, who stumbled. He banged into something with a startled "Ouch!"

Chet spun, shining the beam around. A round, bumpy object flew through the air toward Joe.

He caught it. He stared at it and screamed.

This time there was no mistaking it. In Joe's shaky hands was a bumpy, lumpy human brain!

5

Ghost Story

Joe threw the brain against the wall as hard as he could. The force of his throw knocked him off his feet.

He hit the floor with a thud. He was staring up at the ceiling when something large and white floated over him. Then it covered him up.

"It's alive!" he shouted. "The ghost of Dr. Morrow is alive!"

Joe heard the other boys laughing. Suddenly three smiling faces were looking down at him.

"It's just a sheet that was covering that bookcase," Frank explained, rolling up the sheet.

"Then how do you explain this?" Joe asked, pointing to the brain on the floor.

Frank picked up the brain. "It's not real. It's a model."

"Then why did it attack me?" Joe asked.

"It fell from the top of the bookcase," Frank said. "It was probably holding the sheet in place."

"What about the bony footprints?" Joe asked. "How did they get there?"

"Maybe they were planted to scare us off," Frank said.

"It worked for me," Chet admitted.

"Well, there can't be any ghosts in this room anyway," Mike insisted.

"Why not?" Joe asked.

Mike laughed. "Because it's the living room. Get it? *Living* room."

Frank rolled his eyes. "I get it," he said.

"Can we go now?" Chet asked.

"Why?" Joe asked. "Are you scared?"

Chet grabbed his stomach. "No, I'm hungry. I haven't eaten in over an hour."

"And I'd better return this flashlight to my grandfather before the batteries zonk out," Mike said.

"Boy, what a waste of time," Joe complained as the boys left the house. "No glove, no new suspects. Just a lot of footprints and a bogus brain. How will we ever solve this case?"

"I have an idea. Let's go the library and find that newspaper article," Frank said. "Maybe it will tell us something. See you later, guys."

Mrs. Hardy drove Frank and Joe to the library later that day. She said she would pick them up in half an hour.

The Bayport Library was in a brick building in the middle of town. The boys went straight to the information desk.

"Mr. Kowalski?" Frank asked, looking at the librarian's name tag. "We're looking for a story from the *Bayport Times*."

"Do you know the date?" he asked.

The boys looked at each other. "Um, no," Joe admitted. "But it was the hundredth birthday of the haunted house."

Mr. Kowalski grinned. He wiggled his fingers as if trying to scare them. "Oh, you mean the Morrow mansion."

He stepped out from behind his desk and began to shuffle toward the back of the building like a big monster. "Walk this way," he said in a rough, scary voice.

"Well," Joe whispered, "at least the librarians here know how to have fun."

Mr. Kowalski found the article on microfilm. Then he showed the boys how to use a machine that projected the film on a screen. They could pay to copy any part of it and take the copy home.

"Look!" Joe said. "That's a picture of the house."

The picture showed the house when it was in better condition. At least the windows weren't broken or boarded up. Joe leaned over Frank's shoulder to read the printed story. One word jumped out at him.

" 'Ghost'!" Joe cried, pointing.

Frank read that part out loud. " 'Some people think the Morrow mansion is haunted. The house was built over a hundred years ago by Dr. Samuel Morrow, a prominent surgeon. After his wife died, Dr. Morrow lived there alone with his cat, Winston.' "

"That must be the cat in the portrait," Joe suggested. "Do you think Winston's a ghost now, too?"

"Nah," Frank said. "Cats have nine lives, remember?"

"Very funny," Joe said.

Frank continued reading. " 'When the older Dr. Morrow died, his son, Dr. Robert Morrow, lived in the house. Upon his death, the mansion remained vacant. The house is said to be visited by the ghost of the first Dr. Morrow, who roams the house, dragging his wooden leg.' "

"A wooden leg?" Joe repeated. "I'll bet

that's what made those scratch marks. I told you the place was haunted, Frank!"

"The article says the ghost story is just a rumor," Frank said. But he put in a couple of coins so they could copy the whole page.

"Let's wait for Mom on the front steps," Frank said. "We can read the rest of the article later."

A big stone stairway led up to the library's front door. Joe sat down near the bottom of the steps and looked around.

"Hey, Frank," he said. "Look. There's Biff."

Holding the seat of a pink two-wheeler, Biff was teaching a little girl how to ride her bike. As he ran slowly alongside her on the sidewalk in front of the library, Frank and Joe heard him say, "You can do it. Just look ahead and keep pedaling."

Coming from the other direction on his bike was Zack. He stopped short when he spotted Biff and the girl.

"Isn't that cute?" Zack laughed. "Big bad Biff playing with a little girl!"

"Knock it off," Biff said.

"Come on, let's go to the park," Zack said to Biff. "Or would you rather play with dolls? Ha-ha-ha!"

"I can't go," Biff said. "I promised my mom I'd stay with my cousin."

"What a wimp!" Zack shouted.

Biff's face turned red, but he didn't say anything. That was when Zack looked up and noticed the Hardys.

"Hey! Get a load of Biff, the baby-sitter!" Zack called to Frank and Joe.

"Guess what?" Joe said to Zack. "We were inside the haunted house again today. But we still didn't find the glove."

"Yeah," Frank said. "Maybe somebody just happened to go in and take it out."

Zack snorted. "Maybe Chet got his mommy to get it for him. He's such a wimp." Zack pointed to Biff. "Just like this guy here."

Biff turned to Zack angrily. "I wouldn't talk if I were you. I'm the one who threw Chet Morton's glove in the window for you!"

"Will you shut your mouth, Hooper?" Zack said. He turned his bike around and pedaled away furiously.

"You mean Zack has never been in the house?" Frank asked Biff.

"Read my lips," Biff ordered. "Zack has never gone near the Morrow mansion—ever!"

6

A Bump in the Night

Well, that rules out Zack," Frank said that evening after dinner. He and Joe were back at the computer. Frank pressed the Delete key. "Now we don't have *any* suspects."

"Yes, we do," Joe said. He pointed to the computer screen. "The ghost of Dr. Morrow—or the ghost of his cat."

Frank stared at his computer screen and sighed. "Whatever."

Just then their mom called from downstairs. "Boys? Your friends are here to visit."

Frank turned off the computer. "It must be Chet and Mike," he said.

Chet came through the door, but he wasn't with Mike. He was with a girl. She was a little shorter than Joe, and she was wearing big hoop earrings and a huge turban made from a scarf. She looked like a fortune-teller.

"Who's that?" Joe whispered to Chet.

"It's my crazy sister, Iola," Chet groaned. "I told her about the haunted house. Now she wants to have a séance."

"A say-what?" Frank asked.

"A séance," Iola explained. "That's where we all hold hands and talk to ghosts."

Joe jumped back. "No way! I'm not holding hands with a girl."

"Take it easy," Iola said. "Just think of me as your link to the great beyond."

"Just think of her as a nut," Chet told Frank and Joe.

Joe grabbed Frank's arm. "Frank, let's do it. We have nothing to lose."

Frank scratched his head. He turned to

Iola. "All right. But this doesn't mean I believe in ghosts."

Iola instructed the boys to find four chairs. They set them up around a small table in Frank's room.

"First we turn off all the lights," Iola explained.

"They are off," Joe said. "It's not even dark yet."

"Next we hold hands," Iola said. She grabbed Frank's hand and then Joe's.

"Yuck," Joe muttered.

"Then we close our eyes and picture the spirit of Dr. Morrow," Iola continued.

The boys squeezed their eyes shut.

"What do you all see?" Iola asked.

"The doctor," Frank said slowly.

"The doctor stuffing brains in a jar," Joe answered.

"I see a cheeseburger with pickles and onions," Chet said. "Can we stop now?"

"Be serious," Iola snapped. "Do you want to find your glove or not?"

Joe opened one eye. He stared at Iola. She was swaying back and forth.

"Dr. Morrow!" Iola called out. "If you are with us, give us a sign. Any sign."

Joe opened one eye. "If he's not there, ask for his cat."

Bump!

Frank and Joe jumped.

"What was that?" Frank gasped.

"This is too weird," Chet said.

Frank could feel Iola's hand. It was shaking like a leaf.

Iola gulped noisily. Then she went on. "Dr. M-m-morrow? Is that you?"

Frank and Joe held their breath.

Bump! Bump! Bump!

Chet jumped up from his chair. "I'm getting out of here!" he screamed as he ran from the room.

"Me, too!" Iola cried, running after her brother.

"But you were just getting somewhere!" Joe shouted to Iola.

Iola put her hand on her forehead and

swayed shakily. "Madame Iola is getting another sign. It's from my mom, and she wants me to come home right away."

Frank and Joe could hear Chet and Iola thundering down the stairs and out of the house.

Bump! Bump!

There it was again!

Joe turned to his brother. "That was definitely a sign from the great beyond."

Frank ran his hand against the wall. The bumps sounded as if they were coming from outside.

"Sure. If the great beyond just happens to be our backyard," Frank said.

They ran to the window and looked out. A tall boy with dark hair and glasses was throwing a ball against the house.

Frank and Joe ran down the stairs and out the back door.

"Hey! What are you doing?" Joe called to the boy.

The boy looked at Frank and Joe. Then he began to run.

"Sorry," he shouted over his shoulder. "I thought this house was still vacant."

Frank looked down at the ground. The kid had dropped his baseball glove.

"Wait. You forgot this," Frank called, picking it up. Then he saw something that made his heart race. Marked on the glove in black ink were the initials C.M.

Frank stared at the glove. C.M.: Chet Morton. Could this be the stolen glove? Who was this kid?

The boy dashed back and he grabbed the glove from Frank's hand. "Thanks!" he said. Then he disappeared behind the house next door.

7

Furry Thief

I'm telling you, Joe, that kid might be the baseball-glove thief!" Frank said the next morning. He turned on the computer and added "Mystery kid" to his list of suspects.

Joe shrugged. "Maybe he is, maybe he isn't."

"Then why do you want to search the Morrow mansion again?" Frank asked.

"Because we still haven't ruled out ghosts," Joe explained. "And today I'll get some evidence."

Joe held up a piece of tracing paper.

"What's that for?" Frank asked.

"I'm going to trace the footprints we saw on the floor yesterday," Joe said, "so I can prove that they were made by a skeleton."

"Are Chet and Mike going with you?" Frank asked.

Joe shook his head. "Chet is still spooked from last night. Mike has a dentist appointment."

"Then wait for me," Frank said. "I want to come."

A few minutes later Frank and Joe were heading toward the Morrow mansion. As they turned onto Oak Street, Frank stopped in his tracks. There on the block was the mystery kid. He was wearing the baseball glove and tossing a ball up in the air as he walked.

"That's the kid we saw last night," Frank whispered as the boy turned the corner. "Let's follow him."

Joe nodded. Frank held a finger to his

lips to let Joe know they should be quiet. Then the two boys raced silently around the corner.

The street was deserted. No cars. No kid. "I can't believe it," Frank said. "Where'd he go so fast?"

"I don't know," Joe said, "but forget about him. Let's go to the house."

The brothers walked back to Oak Street and entered the Morrow mansion.

"I'm glad Dad unpacked the flashlight," Frank said as they opened the door. He flicked on the light and shone it at the floor.

"Look!" Joe cried, pointing down. "These are fresh footprints. They weren't here yesterday."

Frank studied the tracks. The prints led down the entrance hall of the mansion toward the back of the house.

"Let's follow them," Frank said.

Joe knelt down on the dusty floor with his tracing paper and a pencil. "Not until I get what I came for."

He carefully traced three footprints. Then he stood up and followed his brother.

The tracks finally led to the kitchen. In it was a wood-burning stove and an old refrigerator. Suddenly the boys heard a faint chattering sound.

"What's that?" Frank hissed.

"I don't know, but it's coming from behind the stove."

The chattering got louder. Then the boys saw something that made their blood run cold. A pair of red eyes stared out at them from behind the stove.

With a shaky hand, Frank aimed the flashlight at the eyes. Then both boys froze. A furry creature leaped out at them. And it was angry!

"It's the ghost of Dr. Morrow's cat!" Joe cried.

The creature let out a squeak. Then it turned and ran back behind the stove.

"Whatever it is, I don't think it likes us," Frank added.

"Don't think—just run!" Joe said.

The boys slid on the dusty floor as they dashed out of the house. They slammed the door behind them and ran the rest of the way home.

"That was quick," Mrs. Hardy said when Frank and Joe burst into their own house.

The boys took a minute to catch their breath. "Have we unpacked the CD-ROMs for the computer?" Frank asked, still gasping.

"Not yet," Mrs. Hardy said. "They're in a carton under the desk."

"Thanks, Mom." Frank headed for the den, followed by a curious Joe.

"What are you doing?" Joe asked.

"Do you still have the footprints you traced at the house?" Frank wanted to know.

Joe pulled the folded paper from his pocket and handed it to Frank.

Frank unfolded the paper and placed it on the desk next to the computer. He opened the box of computer CDs and flipped through them until he found the disc he wanted.

The computer screen soon glowed with the title of the disc Frank had chosen.

"The City Kid's Guide to Nature," Joe read. "What does this have to do with ghosts or skeletons?"

"Nothing," Frank said. "It has to do with animals."

Photos of a deer and a coyote flashed by on the screen. Then came a mountain lion.

"Bingo!" Frank cried. The screen showed a large headline: "Tracks and Trails of North American Animals."

The pictures appeared on the screen. Joe saw the sharp hoofprints of a deer. Then came the padded-paw print of a wolf.

Frank kept working at the computer.

"Stop!" Joe shouted. "There's our footprint. What does it say?"

Frank read slowly. *"Procyon lotor—* the American raccoon."

Joe studied the tracks on the computer screen. "Are you sure?"

"Joe, these look exactly like the prints you traced," Frank insisted. "Who else could they belong to?"

Joe shrugged. "A ghost?"

"A raccoon?" Mrs. Hardy said when the boys told her. "Now I know we're not in the city anymore."

Mr. Hardy shook his head. "Raccoons can turn up anywhere. And they can be dangerous."

"I thought raccoons only fought when they were attacked," Frank said. "That's what it said on the CD."

"Raccoons will also attack when they're scared," Mr. Hardy answered. "And you boys could have scared him."

"The poor thing," Mrs. Hardy said. "He's probably been stuck in that old house for a long time."

"There must be an animal control office in Bayport. They'll know what to do with

59

the raccoon," Mr. Hardy said. "I'll call and see if someone can meet me at the Morrow mansion in half an hour."

"I'll call Chet and Mike," Joe said. "Then we can all go in and watch."

Mr. Hardy firmly shook his head. "You boys will have to wait outside. Let the experts handle the raccoon."

"Right," Joe said. "If it really *is* a raccoon."

Frank and Joe watched as their dad went into the mansion. He was with two workers from the Bayport Animal Control Office.

"I hope Chet and Mike show up soon," Joe said. "This is going to be good."

Suddenly they heard a voice behind them. "Hi again," it said.

Frank and Joe spun around. It wasn't Chet or Mike. It was the mystery kid.

"Neat house, huh?" the kid asked. "I've been inside a couple of times."

Frank thought of Chet's glove. He faced

the boy head-on. "Where did you get that new baseball glove?"

"Huh? My baseball glove?"

Just then Mike and Chet came running into the yard.

"Hey, I see you've met my bro," Mike said.

"Your bro?" Frank asked slowly.

Mike put his arm around the mystery kid's shoulder. "Yeah, my big brother, Carlos."

"Carlos Mendez?" Joe asked.

Frank remembered the initials on the baseball glove. "C.M.?"

Carlos stared at the Hardys. He shook his head. "You guys are weird."

Frank smiled at Carlos. The mystery kid was no longer a mystery. And no longer the glove thief.

Just then the door to the mansion swung open. Mr. Hardy came out followed by one of the animal control officers. She was carrying a cage. Inside the cage was the creature from behind the stove.

The boys stared into the cage.

"It's a raccoon all right," Frank said.

The raccoon blinked at them. It didn't look angry anymore, just tired and scared.

"It *is* a raccoon," Joe said with a sigh. He was disappointed that it wasn't a ghost.

"Oh, boys," Mr. Hardy said. "I found something else."

"What?" Joe asked. "A laboratory with monster parts? A vampire's coffin?"

Mr. Hardy laughed and shook his head. He reached into his jacket and pulled out a baseball glove.

"Does this belong to anyone?"

8

Fools and Ghouls

My glove!" Chet cried. "Thanks. Where was it?"

"It was behind the stove with the raccoon," Mr. Hardy explained. He handed the glove to Chet.

"How did the glove get all the way back there?" Joe wondered out loud.

Frank thought for a moment. Then he snapped his fingers. "I get it! Remember Chet said he was eating a tuna fish sandwich when the Zack Pack took his glove?"

The boys nodded.

"The raccoon probably smelled the tuna on the glove. And a raccoon could have made those scrape marks on the floor when it was dragging the glove away."

Chet put on his glove and smiled. "Well, I'm sure glad to have my glove back." He sniffed it. "Even if it does smell kind of funky now."

Mr. Hardy laughed. He turned to his sons. "Congratulations on solving the case, guys."

"*You* found the glove, Dad," Frank said.

"But you boys found the culprit—the raccoon," Mr. Hardy said. "What do you say we celebrate with a round of ice cream?"

"Sounds great, Dad," Frank said. "But Joe and I don't know any ice-cream places around here yet."

Chet stepped forward. He put his hand on Frank's shoulder. "You guys take care of the mysteries. I'll take care of the snacks. Follow me."

Chet led the way to his favorite ice-cream store, Flavor-a-Day.

While the boys were eating their cones, Mr. Hardy made a phone call.

"I'm glad you got your glove back," Frank said to Chet. "But what about the guys who threw it in there?"

"I know what you mean," Mike said. "It's not fair. They always get away with picking on us."

"Not this time," Frank said. "I've got a plan."

The next morning Frank and Joe ran to the playground.

"Zack! Biff!" Joe called when they got there. "Chet went into the Morrow mansion an hour ago, and he still hasn't come out!"

Zack was busy sticking a spider tattoo on his arm. "Maybe he can't fit through the door," he said with a sneer.

"Besides," Biff said, digging his sneaker toe into the dirt, "what do you want us to do about it?"

"We want you to help us find him," Frank said. "After all, you're the toughest guys in Bayport. No ghosts would mess with you."

Zack grinned from ear to ear. "You got that right!"

Biff looked at Frank and Joe. "I told you guys. Zack won't go near that house."

Zack glared at Biff. "Oh, yeah? Watch me!" He whistled for Mark and Brett. Then Zack and his pack headed for the mansion. As they marched down Oak Street, Joe and Frank talked about Dr. Morrow's ghost.

"The ghost must have gotten Chet," Joe said. "What are we going to do?"

"If you're so worried about Chet, why didn't you go in after him yourself?" Zack said.

"Because we looked in the window,

and we didn't like what we saw," Frank said.

"Bunch of wimps!" Zack said.

When they reached the mansion, the boys walked through the gate. Frank noticed that Zack let all his friends go first.

"So what did you see?" Zack demanded.

Frank walked to the side of the house. "Look for yourself," he said, pointing to the broken window.

"It's dark in there," Brett said.

"Aw, it's just a lot of shadows," Biff said. "But I think someone's lying on the floor."

"What?" Zack shouted.

"Where?" Mark gasped, looking in the window.

Brett looked in, too. "There's a body! And it's not moving!"

"Let's check it out," Zack said.

"I'm not going in there." Biff shook his head.

"What do you mean?" Zack said.

"I don't have a good feeling about this," Biff answered.

Zack's face turned red. "Hey, I'm the leader around here, remember? I'm telling you for the last time, creep, we're going in!"

"You're right about one thing," Biff shouted back. "That's the last time you're telling me to do *anything*. If you're dumb enough to want to go in there, go ahead. But you're not getting me to go along!"

"Fine!" Zack sneered at Biff. "Stay out here like a loser. But we're going in. Right, guys?"

Biff sat down on the front steps while Mark, Brett, and Zack went inside. Frank and Joe quietly followed.

They could hear the Zack Pack ahead of them. Their shouts were hard to miss.

"Ow!"

"Quit pushing!"

"I found a doorway!" Zack yelled over the others. "It must lead to the room with the body." He grunted as he pushed open the door.

"Hey!" Brett called out. "That looks like Morton lying there!"

"What's that wet stuff on the floor around him?"

Zack's voice began to quaver. "Looks like b-b-b-blood!"

His words were cut off as an eerie laugh echoed through the house.

Frank and Joe could see the Zack Pack freeze. Zack clutched Mark's arm. "There's no such thing as ghosts, right?"

"Hey, let go of me," Mark said, shoving Zack.

"Mwah, hah, hah, haaaaaa!" a creepy, whispery voice said. "Come, now. There's no need to be frightened."

Zack looked around. "Who said that?"

As the laughter continued, a rattling skeleton suddenly flew through the air. It hung over the Zack Pack.

"*Aaaaaaagh!*"

"*Eeeeeeeee!*"

"What's the matter, boys?" the voice came again. "Do you need a hand?"

A pasty white hand suddenly came crawling into the room. It moved toward the Zack Pack like a spider.

Screaming their lungs out, the Zack Pack ran for their lives. Zack was right in front, screaming the loudest.

As the screams died away outside, Joe and Frank began to laugh. Then Chet sat up and laughed, too.

Biff came running into the house. "What's going on? What happened to those guys?"

Mike Mendez jumped out from behind one of the dusty chairs, a microphone in his hand. Chet got up off the floor. He carefully stepped around the pool of fake blood.

"A waste of good ketchup," Chet complained, licking his fingers.

"I think that fixed Zack and his pals," Mike said.

"Great work, Mike," Chet said. "That was even better than the robot you made for the science fair."

Frank, Joe, and Mike told Biff the whole story.

"Mike tied the skeleton to a fishing rod and attached the line to the ceiling," Frank explained.

"Then all I had to do was let out the line to make it look like it was floating," Mike went on.

"And this hand is just a white glove with newspaper stuffed in the fingers," Joe told Biff, pointing to it.

"I stuck one of my old wind-up cars inside the glove to make it move," Mike finished.

"It looks pretty real," Biff said, picking up the glove. Then he began to laugh.

Frank, Joe, Chet, and Mike laughed, too. Biff wasn't a creep. In fact, he was neat!

"Well, the case of the missing baseball glove is officially closed," Frank said.

Joe turned to Biff. "By the way. Sorry I made fun of your name the other day. Sorry I punched you, too."

Biff frowned for a second. "Just don't do it again." He laughed and playfully punched Joe in the shoulder.

"Thanks, you guys," Chet said. "You really are good detectives."

"Yeah," Mike added. "You're so good that you need an official name. Let's see. . . ."

"How about the Hardy-har-har Brothers," Chet said.

"What do you think of the Clues Dudes?" Mike asked. "No, wait, I've got it—the Clues Brothers."

"The Clues Brothers," Frank repeated.

"Sounds cool," Chet said.

Frank and Joe nodded.

"All right," Joe said, giving his brother a high five. "I think we're going to like it here in Bayport."

TAKE A RIDE
WITH THE KIDS ON BUS FIVE!

Natalie Adams and James Penny have just started
third grade. They like their teacher, and they like
Maple Street School. The only trouble is, they have
to ride bad old Bus Five to get there!

#1 THE BAD NEWS BULLY
Can Natalie and James stop the bully on Bus Five?

#2 WILD MAN AT THE WHEEL
When Mr. Balter calls in sick,
the kids get some strange new drivers.

#3 FINDERS KEEPERS
The kids on Bus Five keep losing things.
Is there a thief on board?

#4 I SURVIVED ON BUS FIVE
Bad luck turns into big fun
when Bus Five breaks down in a rainstorm.

BY MARCIA LEONARD
ILLUSTRATED BY JULIE DURRELL

A MINSTREL® BOOK

Published by Pocket Books

1237-04

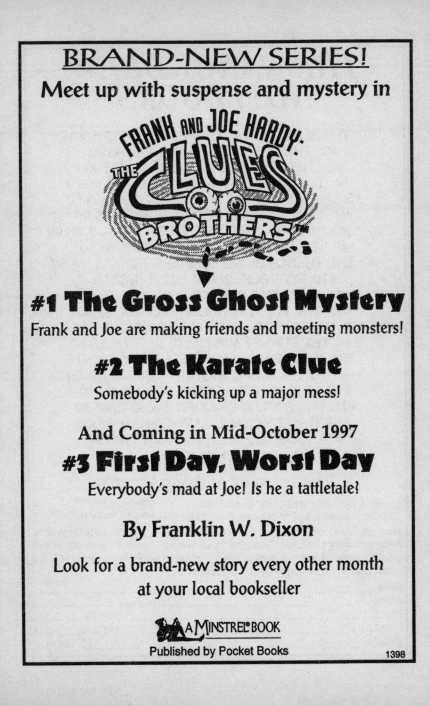

THE NANCY DREW NOTEBOOKS®

by Carolyn Keene
Illustrated by Anthony Accardo

Simon & Schuster Mail Order Dept. BWB
200 Old Tappan Rd., Old Tappan, N.J. 07675   A MINSTREL BOOK
Published by Pocket Books

Please send me the books I have checked above. I am enclosing $_____ (please add $0.75 to cover the postage and handling for each order. Please add appropriate sales tax). Send check or money order--no cash or C.O.D.'s please. Allow up to six weeks for delivery. For purchase over $10.00 you may use VISA: card number, expiration date and customer signature must be included.

Name _____

Address _____

City _____ State/Zip _____

VISA Card # _____ Exp.Date _____

Signature _____

1045-14